T0131643

Black Forest Rain

Elkay

authorHOUSE®

AuthorHouse™
1663 Liberty Drive
Bloomington, IN 47403
www.authorhouse.com
Phone: 1 (800) 839-8640

Published by AuthorHouse 12/03/2015

ISBN: 978-1-5049-6571-2 (sc)
ISBN: 978-1-5049-6569-9 (hc)
ISBN: 978-1-5049-6570-5 (e)

Library of Congress Control Number: 2015919745

Print information available on the last page.

Any people depicted in stock imagery provided by Thinkstock are models, and such images are being used for illustrative purposes only. Certain stock imagery © Thinkstock.

This book is printed on acid-free paper.

CONTENTS

INTRODUCTION

"Black Forest Rain" is a fictional story of a hidden dimension now found. The dimension is "the black forest" where there is unique rain. When it rains it pours and it's not always the same rain.

You are probably asking yourself why this dimension consisting of "the black forest" has never been found until now. Many, many, wonders escaped our knowing for centuries. Each was found due to ironic situations that coincided with the wonder and allowed us to find and unveil its mystery. The same applies to the black forest rain dimension.

An example of another dimension that you may be familiar with is the "bermuda triangle". Over 2,000 vessels and planes have disappeared over time without proven explanation in this dimension. Another dimension is the one connected to the, "loch ness monster". Where else could a monster of this colossal size disappear to?

The controversy over the "Bermuda Triangle" and the "Loch Ness Monster" is as vague and mysterious today as it was when first found. A hidden dimension for each of these anomalies would explain many things about both.

The "black forest rain" also holds differences. This makes it mysterious in its own realm, "the black forest rain dimension".

Our story of "the black forest rain" begins in the "grand canyon" but where does it end? This unanswered question may take ages to uncover but one thing is for sure; it all starts here in this book.

Is there a connection between the "grand canyon" and "the black forest"?

Where did the giant condor bird seen in the "grand canyon" with its 9 feet wing spread originate from? Where did all the bones from the reptiles that died in the "grand canyon" disappear too? Is the "grand canyon" the only place the "colorado river" flows through?

As the author, i know all about the "black forest rain" and will tell you that it's occupied with all kinds of things such as trees with a gigantic canopy on top. The dimension is occupied with forest dwellers and unusual animal creatures that feed on the vegetation and – well, let's leave it at that for now. And also, let's not forget about the black forest rain. Why is it called, "the black forest rain"? is there any light in this dimension? is there day and night? How big is the hidden dimension? This book contains the answers and so much more. It's time to end this introduction and let you get to the story in hand.

Enjoy!

"MAIN CHARACTER INTRODUCTION"

Our story starts on a large privately owned island where our main book character is born and raised. He is raised as an only child by extremely wealthy parents in a castle on a remote island near the United States. His birth was a hard one. Everyone thought he was lost because he was so weak and tiny. He struggled for life and beat the odds. He was born two weeks early. His name is "Victor". How ironic is his name. He was victorious with dispelling conflict and conquering life after birth. The island is self sufficient in every respect. The staff includes all possible needs such as tutors, chefs, maids, waiters, trainers in sports, etc. All staff personnel must be under 25 years of age and genius in their field of expertise. Those turning 23 were marked for retirement at age 25 as millionaires and substitutes hired to become their replacements. His parents did not want to accept any liability for anyone over 25 years of age. Victor enjoyed trips and vacations to the United States and elsewhere. His island home was a paradise but his isolation instilled a possessed yearning for learning at a very young age and never weakened. His favorite pastime was inspecting the castle from top to underneath and exploring the 15 mile radius island.

His parents released him to American universities when he became college age. the young bachelor had dedicated hobbies and ambition in obtaining master degrees associated with scientific travel, research, and discovery.

He always returned to his island castle and paradise during college breaks and whenever else he could. He would use his return visits to continue exploring the castle, island, and abroad.

It was on one of his abroad explorations that victor's life would change forever.

CHAPTER 1

A Hidden Dimension Is Found

A fire breaks out in one of the deepest parts of the "grand canyon". The only way to get to it is by dropping fire fighters by helicopter. Three fire fighters with full gear and fire fighting equipment are a full load for the helicopter. The pilot charts a course and finds that the area in flames is remote and uncharted; however, the strong winds can only fuel the fire below and make for an even worse situation. The only thing reported thus far to the fire station was the huge amount of black smoke pushing upward toward the suspecting tourists. This makes the situation extremely urgent and highly serious so the fire fighters decide to move out with haste even though no one had yet reported seeing flames.

Approaching the fire point, each fire fighter secures their portion of the fire equipment and jumps out each in turn. The fire fighters maneuver themselves directly over and center of the black smoke as they plummet downward. Down and down they go. They start to realize that the fire is contained within the walls of a huge hole. They continue down until they finally get to the bottom. So deep is their descent that the oxygen is scarce and causing few flames but much smoke. The fire fighters put on their oxygen masks and quickly start to battle the flames. Two of the three fire fighters are lost to the flames. The third and youngest firefighter continues to fight but soon realizes the flames are out of control. The firefighter grabs as much gear as he can carry and backs up against the rocks. The firefighter can barely tolerate the intense heat from the growing flames. He tugs on the lifeline from the helicopter hovering far above.

The helicopter pilot responds quickly. He engages the life line hoist and starts pulling the fire fighter out of harms way.

As the firefighter rises towards the helicopter, he looks down and believes for a second that he notices a lone figure which immediately disappears in the black smoke. The firefighter keeps looking but never sees the figure again. He knows his eyes had to be playing tricks as no one could survive this fire from hell. The firefighter is safely recovered but deeply saddened by the lost of his fellow firefighters. The creed of firemen and firewomen is never to abandon your comrades; as such, the helicopter continues to be endangered until both demised firefighters are recovered. The jaw device was attached to the end of the hoist and released to the ground. The jaw settled onto the firefighter, closed, and then retrieved. The same was quickly done for the other demised firefighter.

The helicopter is badly singed but pulls off and out of the smothering fire. The pilot noticed the first saved firefighter never took his eyes off the fire site and was still looking back. He asked why he was so transfixed on the fire location. The other firefighter says he thought he saw a moving figure when he was being saved but a second look showed nothing. His eyes must have been playing tricks on him. If anything was still alive down there it had to be animal because a human could not have survived. Even though he had convinced himself as such, he still focused during the time they recovered the lost two firefighters. He was not satisfied that there was no one else left below.

He nor anyone else will ever know that the imagined lone figure below was real.

The lone figure was not one of the tourist but our young bachelor (victor) on exploration from his remote island and now in a Grand Canyon fire.

Unfortunately, one of the tourists above his level dropped a finished lit cigarette. It quickly ignited the dry brush below and soon reached the damp wood and other brush causing fire and black smoke in victor's area. He was able to reach the canyon wall before the smoke strangled him into unconsciousness. He quickly put on his trench coat as a cover against the choking smoke and heat from the burning fire. He buried his head inside the trench coat but it still didn't stop his passing out. Lying still and flat against the canyon wall concealed him from sight when the firefighters arrived on the scene. Luckily, victor woke in time to escape the deadly smoke and fire. The trench coat had absorbed enough air to revive victor for only a few moments. He saw a crevice behind burned out foliage in the wall only a few feet away. Crawling over and up he squeezed into the small opening.

The opening was very dark at the back making it appear to be only a few feet deep. As victor grabs hold of his backpack and squeezes to the back of the entrance he suddenly starts to fall downward. He hits his head upon falling into the dark unknown. The hit was mild enough that it makes him dizzy and disoriented. He is still conscious enough to realize he is falling like a feather. The air is very thick and makes it difficult to breathe. He continues to fall and his trench coat fills with the air and acts as a parachute. As he descends the fall becomes faster and finally makes victor pass out. Victor finally hits the bottom. His unconsciousness and the make do parachute from the trench coat prevents victor from incurring any serious injury. Being unconscious made his body totally relaxed; as such, the impact was absorbed without any serious injuries. His relaxed state made his body flexible enough to protect bone breakage.

Hours come and go until victor finally awakes to find himself removed from the "grand canyon" deep fire pit. He was now somewhere else. He could see light way up above in the crevice but not for long.

As he looked, he watched the crevice slowly close and the outside light fade away. He was now locked in to who knows where. He was disturbed, confused, and lost. Lost to what? His recollection of the outside world had been taken from him. He was conscious of the "Grand Canyon" ordeal that placed him in his present location; otherwise, he was the victim of selective amnesia. He would find out that he retained memories that would be needed for survival in his present state but no memories of his past that gave him any desire to escape. The life that had made him an extraordinary man of health, strength, education, exploration, and search for knowledge had been lost. "Victor" was still fully functional without knowing how.

For whatever reason, the atmosphere provided the right makeup to allow easy breathing and movement. How was this possible? Staying where he was would not give him any answers. he would have to explore his surroundings. he first made a permanent marker where he was at. This would show him where to return if he had to and also keep him from traveling in circles. Victor would soon find out that he had accidentally found the hidden entrance to a dimension strapped to the earth. The crevice was prided open by the shift in the land plate that centers on the earth and dimension. During his capture in this hidden dimension, victor would find that this occurrence happens once a year.

The constant banging of the earth ocean waters loosens the land plate and shifts it on its pedestal. It takes one year for the hammering ocean water to fully move the land plate to its other side.

The dimension was its own hidden territorial space with an unusual composition. the dimensional space was transparent and not visible as other outer space was. This dimension was space within space. The dimension composition properties makes the inner dimensional space dark black. The dimension also emits invisible floating dust. There is only one world within the dimension. It became the dimensions only world because its compositional make-up matches the composition of the dimensions invisible dust in a negative manner. The dust has a positive composition make-up and the floating dead world has a negative compositional make-up. The occurrence of pulling the floating dead world into the hidden dimension happened because of the magnetic pull between the two. The invisible floating dust stuck on the passing dead world as it passed by and locked it in the dimension. The dead world was now a permanent and invisible part of the dimension. The absorbed dead world took up the majority of the dimensions space. Anything else with the same composition make-up as the dead world and invisible dust had would have to be very small to pass inside the dimension and be locked onto. There was no room for anything big to ever enter. Also, most of the invisible floating dust was now stuck on the dead world. The remaining dust could only stick onto something very small passing the dimension. The dead world was now in a locked position to allow it to come to life. It would later become alive.

The earth ocean waters would flow into the strapped dead world. The constant years of shift and rubbing of the earth ground plates under the earth oceans had made a tear opening. The opening started allowing earth ocean waters and occupants into the dead world. Many of the incoming occupants were living organisms. These living organisms thrived in their new home and became the animal, mineral, and vegetables. The dead world was now a live world.

There was limited light created by an absorbed sponge like moon and the reflections bouncing off the ceiling ice prisms.

The moon had similar properties as the inner world did. As the moon passed into the world it was immediately trapped in place. The moon make-up acted like a negative pull to the positive similar make-up of the inner world. The inner world's magnetic pull drew the passing object into it. The object was locked to the inner world ceiling and never to leave. it was the first permanent fixture in the inner world. The light closest to the ceiling produced beautiful multi-colored light. The ice prisms are in many colors created from the water entry from earth and traveling down different core veins to the inner world ceiling. Each vein had a mysterious mineral make-up that changed the water to a color that had its own power application. These power colors come from the mixing of the invisible dust in the earth waters. Both stir together as they pass through many veins leading to the inner world ceiling.

Another object that passed into the invisible dimension space was a huge rubberized spinning blanket. It also possessed the unusual make-up of the inner world and invisible dust. The spinning rubberized blanket was caught by the inner world.

The spinning motion stretched the rubberized blanket as it spun around the inner world. It finally encased the entire inner world. The material properties of the rubberized blanket made it impervious to penetration. Any passing objects that would otherwise be dangerous, destructive, or worse would simply be repelled on contact. The magnetic element in the rubberized blanket, which had been cloaked over the inner world, had the opposite affect on everything else. All matter that neared the cloak would be dispelled before contact. The single inner world was well protected.

CHAPTER 2

Black Forest Rain

How ironic that a dimension should coexist with our earth. There is one region within the dimension called "the black forest". The region is scarred from bad black rain but also flourishes from good pure rain".

The rain comes from two sources. The first comes from the earth ocean waters that cross over the dimension tear and flow down the inner world veins until the water (containing small dirt and sand particles) reaches the ceiling. The particles of sand and dirt fall to the floor before the incoming waters freeze on the ceiling. This has made a fertile ground floor over the centuries. Other occupants within the incoming waters fall to the ground also. Most are living organisms that become the inner worlds animal, mineral, and vegetable. the water stops and freezes on the dimensions inner world ceiling. The freeze is caused by the cold incoming water getting colder and colder as it passes down the dark cold dimension inner world core veins. Each vein has a different mysterious core ingredient. The captured ocean water mixes with the core ingredient and becomes a powerful frozen tonic. Each tonic property has its own magical power and color. All the core veins pass through the same canal and then separate into their own as they finally settle on the ceiling. The colors mix as they spread out on the ceiling creating multiple colors of ceiling prisms and crystals. a very unusual occurrence has taken place since the beginning of the earth waters entering the dimension.

There are a couple of pebbles lying at the end of the canal where the core colors emerge from.

The core colors sometimes loose a speck of their core color as they travel. These specks are absorbed individually into two pebbles at the end of the canal; as such, nature comes in and creates a pebble with all the colors imbedded individually. This one pebble contains all the powers. The other pebble has many but not all of the color specks. The pebbles shook off during a one time earth quake that breached the dimension for a couple of seconds and caused the incident. The earth quake took place in the Grand Canyon area where the crevice appears once a year. The earthquake is so intense that the vibrations reverberate through the closed crevice crack.

The contained power in each color is noted below.

Light red is power to burn anything

Light yellow is strength

Light blue is power to control water

Light brown is power to implode things

Light orange is power to levitate things

Light green is power to move ground

Light white is power of magic
Light bronze is power to give flight
Purple is power of invincibility
Crystal clear is power of invisibility
Dark blue is power to change shape
Dark green is power to transport oneself
Pink is poison power and kills instantly.

Pale orange hides the color being used and keeps the skin color its normal appearance.

The "black forest" exists because the floor of this dimension region allows growth and life. The dimension has a region at one end of the black forest that is different in makeup.

This region appears lifeless and made of caves with bald and desolate floors. This region was created from falling meteors and such before the inner world was captured by the hidden dimension.

This is the only known region that is non-magnetic; as such, passing objects were able to drop and settle in this area of the dead world. Unlike earth, the dimension doesn't turn or have any movement in the space it occupies.

The area where the "black forest" is located has a fixed sponge like globe. It is locked below the dimension ceiling. The drifting sponge like object was also absorbed in the falling dimension from passing space. It is big enough to provide a cover of sufficient heat and light to the "Black Forest" region. The heat is generated from the chemical makeup in the bottom of the sponge. The chemicals also glow and help produce a small amount of constant light for the "Black Forest". The top side of the rectangular sponge has no chemical makeup and stays dark and cold. The floor of the "black forest" emits an invisible vapor that rises to the sponge like globe and changes to water. The vapor comes from the indigenous burnt vegetation caused by the black acid rain.

The water provides constant nourishment to the globe who in turn releases the excess back to the "Black Forest". A lot of the water picks up an acid makeup from the globe chemicals and charred vegetation. The excess water falls down as black acid rain.

The entire dimension is encased with a blanket of black coated substance to shield it from the outside. The dimension was lifeless space and unprotected until the black rubberized blanket approached and cloaked the inner world. The dimension has survived time where others have perished because the rubberized substance repels anything that comes in contact with it. This protects the inner core of the dimension from all danger and harm. The black blanket is a substance that creates thick vapors from the inner world outer core. The vapors originate from the area between the blanket cloak and the inner world outer core. The vapors permeate into the inner world. They can't pass through the blanket cloak because of its in-penetrating capabilities. The incoming vapors are absorbed in the "Black Forest" sponge like globe. The vapors are nourishment to the sponge and become water. Some of the vapors escape the sponge like globe and rise back to the rubberized blanket. The thick vapors absorb floating particles as it rises and hardens at the top of the inner world. Layers of hardened core and mineral deposits are continuously formed.

Salt water is the magic ingredient that mixes with mineral deposits and produces specific power ability within each of the ceiling frozen color ice prisms. Each color power is produced by mixing with salt water traveling in a core mineral vein. As the incoming salt water freezes into a colorful ice prism as it settles on the ceiling.

Salt is a substance of non-existence in the dimension but nature takes care of itself and introduces earth ocean salty waters to the dimension "black forest" ceiling. For some unknown reason the salty water permeates through the rubberized blanket, down the frigid core mineral levels and veins, and freezes on the ceiling. As it slowly melts, the drops fall as black acid rain. This is the downside of the made magic. With so much being mixed together, the resulting water color turns black when melted and falls as black acid rain. The falling drops lose 99% of their magic power. The remaining 1% helps the vegetation it touches to live longer before turning into black charred habitat. Falling drops are so few at one time that they are undetectable unless being directly seen when falling; as such, it will be way in the future before one discovers these falling rain drop events.

Rain showers are produced from the swelled sponge-like globe. The globe absorbs the thick vapors from the dimensions inner world ceiling. When the sponge becomes overfilled it will release the excess as rainfall. It then returns to its normal size and repeats the process. Each rain shower is a mixture of clear rain and black rain. The water falling from the sponge top is good rain and the water falling from the bottom is bad rain (Black Acid Rain).

There are trees with canopy tops that are immune from the falling black acid raindrops; as such, anything under the tree canopies is shielded and protected.

The good rain gives needed nourishment to the ground and inhabitants. This allows the plants, trees, flowers, etc. to grow and expand.

Then there is the bad rain. It covers the forest environment with black coating, thus creating the black forest effect and other unfortunate occurrences. All of the black rain has an acid makeup and scars/burns anything if touches.

As such, the life forms find shelter in the "black forest" tree covers and the baron caves at the end of the "black forest" for protection during rain showers.

The clear rain bestows endless wonders within the black forest. The first and probably most important effect of the good rain is its seeping into the dimension floor and turning it into a soft fertile bed for the growing habitat. The good rain also creates pools of crystal clear purified water for drinking and other uses by the inhabitant life forms.

Nature somehow intervened and added open veins on the big canopy leaves. the falling black rain would land in the veins and mix with the veins substance make-up; thereby, changing the black rain to pure and clear water that lands on the "Black Forest" floor.

The good water brings a pulse to the "Black Forest" and with passing time living organisms develop and grow. These organisms become different kinds of fish life in the water.

These various organisms slowly evolve to bigger and bigger sizes and many become land beings. Some of the black forest inhabitants have a very small brain that initially doesn't function. As the living inhabitants start to recognize their surroundings their brain starts receiving the information and builds from that point. These are the superior beings. The majority have brains that never develops but do function enough to allow understanding orders from the superior ones.

Over time, a few of the life forms fed on the rare poison black rain pools and mutated into scary life forms some of which are nice and some not nice. They mimic to what they see and react to how they are reacted to. Some are taken as pets and the remainder used as workers.

The outer region of the dimension "black forest" is made up with caves that touch the borders of our earth oceans. On high tides the ocean waters drift across the outer dimension and seep into the cave ceilings. The water takes on different properties as it slides down the many layers of different mineral deposits of rock. The bitter coldness of total darkness and ocean waters freezes the water as it settles on the cave ceiling.

The penetrating water also takes on different colors from the different mineral veins it follows to the cave ceiling.

The end result is a magnificent beauty of crystallized colors of frozen ocean water. Each color has a unique power and identifying color. the crystallized ocean water forms prisms that reflect off one another and create a dim amount of colorful light visibility on the "black forest region" ceiling.

CHAPTER 3

Victor's First Encounter
With The Black Forest

It's been several days since "Victor" fell into the "Black Forest". The first threat he faced was the black forest rain. Luckily, Victor had already moved himself under a black forest tree canopy which protected him from the damaging black falling rain. As he watched the black rain he saw it burn and scar everything it settled on. Victor had learned several things from his ordeal: The canopy tree not only sheltered him but it was not affected by the down coming rain; in fact, the composition of the tree canopy changed any black rain that touched it to clear water. The black rain had to have an acid makeup that made it a weapon of mass destruction. Many years of damage had changed much of the forest to black matter thereby its name to be "Black Forest".

While the black rain fell, victor made a list of things he needed to do to survive in his new world. At the top of his list was food and water. He would surely perish very quickly without either of these two needs. His water supply was only a few steps from him. the clear rain rolling off the tree canopy had created a pond of clear water. He could see living land around the pond so it must be pure water. Victor decided to make this area secure and safe as his new residence.

Until this moment, victor was incredibly depressed with no hope, desire, or will to live but now he couldn't wait to start his journey and research of this hidden dimension linked to our Earth. This linkage gives victor the hope to survive and find his was back to Earth. His amnesia was gone.

The adrenalin rush and increased heart beat of excitement has triggered his brain and revived his total memory. The black rain stops and victor can now look for food. He steps out from under the tree and trips on an object that turns out to be a vegetable like our earth carrot. He looks up and sees the unusual beauty of the tall and wide tree. Victor chuckles to himself as he looks upon the tree ornaments. He wouldn't have to travel far to find his food supply. The ornaments were various kinds of vegetation. This particular canopy tree produced an oasis of vegetation within its canopy.

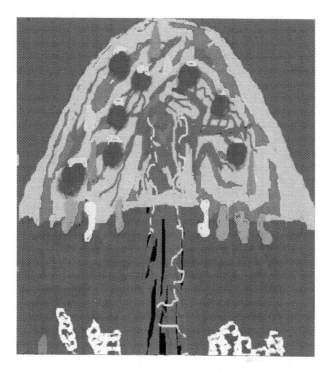

The heavy pouring of rain beating down on the tree canopy loosens the vegetation which will finally break loose and fall to the ground.

This is a good thing because victor had no way of getting to the tree canopy vegetables. He collected all of the falling vegetables to store for later consumption.

Not knowing or having any meat source forces victor to be a vegetarian. Victor drifts back in time for a moment.

He remembers the great times he had hunting for food on the island. Maybe he will somehow encounter hunting times later in this "Black Forest". It was definitely something he looked forward too.

Victor is young and strong but tired and sleepy. He gathers some of the big tree canopy leaves and makes a bed in the holler part of the canopy tree.

Although the vegetable canopy trees are sponge canopies, this particular one has leafs protruding from underneath and outwards. This tree was also much bigger at the base and provided a sunken cave like cavity. It was big enough for victor's bed and storage. Victor settled in for a long sleep to recover his body's strength and health. Victor relaxes his body and stares upward. There is no sky but he is transfixed on the colorful "Black Forest" ceiling. Lying motionless, his intuition tells him something isn't right. It finally dawns on him. There was total silence in his surroundings. Nothing stirred, not even the night air. He was realizing that his prison was like a basketball. It was self contained. The only weather would be rain. There was no environmental makeup like earth to produce snow, hail, lighting, thunder, tornadoes, hurricanes, etc.

He didn't know if this was a good or bad thing. He did surmise that he was the only living person in this dimension.

This didn't trouble victor because he was an only child and very accustomed to being alone. As he drifted into unconsciousness he thought how ironic it was that his life's ambition was exploration, research, and discovery and he had fallen into the biggest find of his life. He doesn't know that this turn of events will alter and change his life forever. He also doesn't know that he is not alone in this dimension.

Victor makes it to the edge of unconsciousness but is then bought back totally awake. Noises are heard coming from the dark. Strange noises but at least one he recognizes; that was the movement of bushes. There was no wind so something else was shaking the brush. He heard stomping noises but couldn't determine what kind.

Victor definitely knows he is far from being alone in this new world. He also knows there will be no sleep for him tonight. The moon gears down every day and causes almost complete darkness. Victor cannot even see his hand in front of his face. He feels completely safe with the darkness being his protector for now. Being afraid doesn't stop victor from becoming very inquisitive about what lives in this area of the dimension. When light appears, victor has decided to investigate the grounds for any signs of life. His body becomes relaxed as he rests. His mind starts to drift back to his island home on earth. He goes into a deep sleep.

CHAPTER 4

"Home Sweet Island Home"

Victor had finally settled in. This inner world was completely different from his earth world. He had not learned much at this time but he was going to. For now he would rest. This was a bazaar setting he was living in but he accepted it. He really had no other choice; as such, he would be the first explorer in this new home. He began thinking of his wonderful life and the island home back on earth. It was his private world and paradise. "Victor" was feeling home sick. He was much different from his other island cousins. They were as their parents, introverts with no desire for the outside world. "Victor" on the other hand was an extreme extrovert with the genes of an adventurer. He didn't think he would ever find anything or anywhere that would touch his heart any better than his island home. His desire was to experience as much of the world as he could and absorb the countless customs, environments, animals, and habitats.

He would keep journals of language recordings and videos. These he would keep organized, safe, and secure for later use. If and when he became unable to travel for whatever reasons, he would fall back on his journals to use as scientific study, writing books, etc.

"Victor's" island home was self-sufficient in every respect. It had been occupied by his family tree for centuries. The island was initially bestowed on his distant grandparent by a Viking king of a far away land. The Vikings were a warrior made people and made constant travels to find fighting ventures and obtain possession of the lands.

"Victor's" island was one of these lands won from an unfortunate tribe that the Vikings made extinct.

The island was all but forgotten about being it was so far away from the Vikings homeland. The Vikings always went in other directions for their adventures which also made the island remote and lost for all causes.

"Victor's" family was linked to a Viking warrior who had two daughters each with husband and boy or girl child. The Viking warrior was one of the king's body security guards. Their job of protecting the king was most difficult when the king accompanied his brave and courageous warriors on special attacks. It was during one of these fighting engagements that the king's life was the main focus of the opposition. The Viking scouts overheard the enemy saying if they killed the king the rest would weaken and be easily overcome. This was very serious information conveyed to the king. Their enemy was notorious for their beastly fighting and had never lost a battle. Wining this battle would be a great prize for the Viking King and render enormous fear and submission far and wide. They would also reap enormous wealth from winning. One of the Viking warrior's was highly loyal to his king and the Viking community. He approached the king and kneeled at his feet. The king asked "what it is you want".

The Viking warrior replied with his head lowered downward, "I want no more than to guarantee your unharmed and safe return to our mother land". I would be honored if you would allow me to be disguised as you. The king was puzzled and wanted to know more. He tells the Viking warrior to rise and sit beside him. The warrior explains how the king would be safe and secure by having someone pretend to be the king during battle attacks. The king admires the sacrifice idea the Viking warrior offers.

He accepts the idea and has the Viking warrior disguised as his look alike. The king only revealed this idea to two of his most loyal warrior guards.

Many small battles came and went with the king being hidden and the warrior imposter taking his place at the battle front. The king had the two loyal warriors hypnotized at the end of each battle. The kings' secret would then be only known by himself and the imposter king. The king would pick the same two other highly loyal warriors on each battle. The big battle finally showed itself. The king prepared his army and informed his people to seek cover until the battle end. The king was hidden and guarded by his two most loyal and skilled warriors. The brave and courageous disguised soldier warrior took his place at the front of the battle. The imposter king fought fearlessly and killed far more enemy warriors than anyone else. His suburb fighting skills set the example for his Viking army who did the same. The enemy king realizes he is losing and directs his strongest and skilled beastly soldiers to concentrate on killing the king. The battle intensifies. The imposter king is surrounded by his warriors as they fight on.

The enemy put up a superb fight but still lost in the end. Not only did the enemy lose but so did the imposter king. He was nearly killed midway in battle. His near death stirred his warrior army into a fighting frenzy. They fought as if possessed and quickly won the war. The incredible brave sacrifice of the imposter king not only saved the real king but allowed the Vikings to win the battle.

Placing their best soldiers to focus on killing the king greatly weakened the remaining enemy. This turned the greater strength to the Vikings who took the day. The Viking king came secretly out of hiding and quickly departed with his Viking army. He didn't want to give the enemy time to regroup for another battle at this time.

The Viking king had accomplished his objective by inserting a deep wound into his enemy. For now, the enemy was convinced they were beaten and glad that the Viking king gave mercy on them by leaving their land. The enemy now feared the Vikings and wanted as much distance between the two as possible.

After their return home, the Viking king immediately assembled his people. He described their ordeal, praised his soldiers, humbled respect and tearful thanks to the dying Viking soldier who sacrificed himself for his king and mother land. The king then ordered a feast be put into play immediately so that they all may celebrate their accomplishments for those soldiers who didn't return and show his appreciation to the dying Viking soldier. The king always admired him more than any other until his dying day. The king asked for silence after several hours into the feast, celebration, and festivities. He had Viking guards place the near dead valiant soldier on the floor in front of him. The king then knelt down, lowered his head, and whispered private words to his unselfish soldier who knew he would be killed but still offered his life for the kings' life. The king then stood up and raised his arms and head upward. He then told everyone to do the same. He then spoke words in honor of the dying soldier with everyone rejoicing. Next, the king then assembled the dying soldiers' family and with them and everyone as witness, says "you are the sole owner from this day forward and forever for the distant uninhabited island measuring 20 miles in any direction. You and yours will never be obligated in any way to me or my country. I am giving you the deed and a gold medallion secured in a steal container with lock and key. The medallion will bear the kings' seal of testament and guarantee to this transaction. The container was large enough to store an abundance of gold coins and other wealth. The king tells the family they have also earned the protection of his soldiers whenever needed.

Simply show the medallion as proof of this Viking commitment. I will send 50 skilled workers and 50 soldiers to be helpers and protectors to build an island fortress and other necessities. Once completed, the soldiers are to return. You may allow up to 5 skilled workers to remain and live out their lives on the island if they so wish. I will have two small vessels secured to the Viking ship for you to keep. They will be equipped with fishing items, tools, weapons, and other materials. Seed was also be supplied to establish initial crops. 10 chickens, 2 hunting dogs, 2 cows, 2 goats, and 4 horses will be given to help with food, hunting, milk, and travel. All this is but a small token of my sincere appreciation". The king then uses his prized knife to cut the palm of his hand. He cuts a line on the dying soldier's forehead. He pressed his palm on the soldiers' forehead and as the blood of the two mixed, the king echoed to all in his presence that he is now honored that this Viking warrior is his blood brother and Viking royalty. The king ended by saying, this is as it should be. He was a king but for a short period but nevertheless a king. With his last breath, the soldier died with the king looking upon him and seeing a smile of thanks.

So that's how the Viking Island came to thrive again with people. The initial occupants were a family of seven; two married couples with one child each and the dead Viking soldier. One of the married women was the only daughter of the dead Viking soldier. She was the only royalty on the island for now. Her children would reign as royalty in the future. "Victor" is one of them.

The imposter Viking kings' daughter was named Jackie. Since she was now royalty, a minor percentage of the Viking kings' gained wealth was sent to her at various times by the king's escort and confidant.

The first thing that was done after reaching the island home was to bury the honored Viking warrior. The daughter "Jackie" asked that a drift be made to carry her father out to sea. The drift was made, the soldier placed upon it, straw placed around the soldier, and the drift pushed off shore.

After the drift was at a distance, an archer released a flaming arrow into the air from the shore line. The flaming arrow found its precise mark to start a ceremonial fire. This is how the Vikings dispose of their dead. Each is honored in this manner.

The islanders disperse and start construction of the island home. Various groups are formed for the tasks needed at hand. "Jackie" selects a location to have a shelter built big enough for all to eat in. She asked the group to determine a time for meals and all do. Three times are selected; one for breakfast, lunch, and dinner.

These times would also be used to account for everyone and discuss any needed matters.

The shelter would be taken down once everything was completed and the main Viking populous returned home.

As time passed, the island and its inhabitants grew in numbers and prospered. Since "Jackie" was royalty, her family owned the island and had final say so on all things. "Jackie's" disposition had always been that of a quiet, shy, and stand-offish. She was very kind and considerate of others. She was a very hard worker.

She may have appeared weak because of her humility and life-style but those around her now know otherwise. She is still the same "Jackie" but shows great courage, strength, and wisdom in leading the island inhabitants. The first building task she asked for was a rock structure built against and into the highest land point. She suggested that everyone work and live together initially.

When the rock structure was completed, those outside her family could scout the island for a home location. They could work at their location anytime they were not on work task at the point. This strategy proved worthwhile and progress moved very rapidly.

When finished, the structure had become an enormous and beautiful castle resting at the highest point on the island. It's construction composition, surrounding barriers, and location made it impenetrable. A wide waterway was made circling the point. The end result provided a private island of many acres.

The inhabitants were given sufficient time to build their homes to include the 5 skilled trade workers who wanted to live out their life on the island. The time finally came and those required to, returned to their Viking mother land. The remaining inhabitants are satisfied with living and staying close to their home. They visit their neighbors and make their presence to the point when asked.

Present day has the island area initially settled and developed into a self-contained paradise. All needed possessions have their own facilities to accommodate the populous. The point approves each and every possession and structure. Non-essential ones such as fast food, toy stores, etc. are disapproved. Even technology is kept to the bare minimum. The inhabitants are totally satisfied with their level of living standards and strive to keep it that way. Trouble makers are secured for examination and investigation.

If their crimes are not caused by mental problems, they are confined to island work and given a rehabilitation chance. Those who do not adjust are removed from the island and warned never to return.

The royal family at the point is somewhat different than the other inhabitants. There lifestyle is that of royalty. The women are introverted with no interest outside the island.

The men are extroverts with intense curiosity and desire for adventure. It's no wonder that "Victor" is the way he is. He is the descendant of a Viking warrior. He comes from royalty. He has inherited a great deal of strength and wisdom from his descendents. Vikings are big built, adventurers, strong and skilled warriors, and quick thinking. "Victor" is all of these and more. There is another interesting point about "Victor". He was born with the luck of the Irish. He was the 7th son of the 7th son. Legend has it that those born in this position are destined to witness great things and carries extreme luck with them throughout their life.

"Victor's" blood line ends with his family. Present day has him, his family, and uncle living on the private estate. It won't be long before he becomes the last one of royalty.

CHAPTER 5

"Black Acid Rain Impact On Dimension"

There are side affects from the "Black Forest Rain". One major effect is the burns endured by the inhabitants and destruction to the land caused by the acidity in the black rain. Most of the "Black Forest" inhabitants are not very smart and have to cope with the acid rain consequences. Many are disfigured with scotched burns and distorted scars because they were unable to avoid the acid rain.

An occurrence of acid rain only lasts a little while but much destruction can happen to both the land and the land beings during these times. The superior land beings have enough sense to come in out of the rain and avoid its poison. The others go for cover after feeling the initial pain from the falling acid rain. These few seconds cause severe damage to any without head cover.

One thing that is immune to the black acid rain is the canopy trees. Their composition makes the black acid rain change to good clear rain. The clear rain drops roll off and drop to the ground. Each canopy tree has a pond that has been created over time from the clear rain drops. The vegetation that grows on the edge of the pond is protected by the canopy tree and escapes the black rain drops. Nothing can survive beyond the canopy tree top. This is why there is so much baron ground in the black forest. There may be areas in the dimension that thrive with vegetation because they are out of the range of the black acid rain drops.

The "black forest" acid rain has also caused some changes in the indigenous creatures. The "Hard Back Carrier" looks like a mixture of ox and horse. It has evolved into a mighty creature with a steal like back that repels anything to include acid rain. This creature is the source of travel for the land beings.

The razor back "Caydough" is a creature that looks like a mixture makeup of cat and dog. It has evolved over time. It is covered with hard but smooth topside that comes to a point. The point is razor sharp and protrudes out beyond the head. This allows the "Caydough" to stab or tear anything harmful to it apart. The smooth topside protects the "Caydough" from falling objects and the acid rain. This creature is the pet, companion, and guardian for the land being.

These are the two primary land creatures used by the land beings to live and survive in the "Black Forest" dimension and also move fast to a cover that avoids the black acid rain.

The inhabitants have learned how to remove the back of both animals.

The back of the "Hard Back Carrier" is mainly shaped into head and shoulder covers to repel the acid rain. This protection allows the wearer to move about during the black acid rain showers. The superior craftsmen have experimented with the hard back and created many working and fighting tools. The "Long Arm" which is the equivalent to earth's spear is one of the favorites. It acts as a walking stick and weapon against predators. It is curved on the top end below the spear head to keep the item or items being carried from falling off. The land beings have learned how to position the "long arm" on their shoulder to balance the load carrying and allow much weight to be carried easy.

The "Caydough's" back is used to make the tools and weapons to work with and protection. Some are made to be smooth and others with jagged edge. The back of the "Caydough" is long enough to accommodate the making of small different shape "Chew's". The earth chew is called a "saw". The "Chew" (earth saw) is attached to a standard handle for cutting purposes.

The organic composition of the "Caydough's" back makes it many times sharper than that of the earth saw's. The superior craftsmen pride themselves with the making of the "Blade Twirl". The "Blade Twirl" is paper thin and as with the "Long Arm", incredibly sharp. There are different sizes but the main "Blade Twirl" is 6 inches round. The primary usage of this tool is to sever the fruit and vegetables from the canopy tree. It is also used to slay animals for food, game entertainment such as target practice, and protection weapon.

There are other land creatures in the "black forest" dimension that will unveil their-self when the occasion calls. Most of the dimension land creatures are unseen because they hide undercover to defend themselves from the acid rain and other "black forest" predators looking for live food.

The land beings stay prepared for hunting these land creatures after an acid rain comes and goes. This hunting time is the easiest because some of the creatures found are those that were wounded or killed by the black acid rain. The wounded are easy kills to use for food and other needs. The other animals also emerge from their protected cover to find food and water. They are then subject to capture or killing. These animals become pets, working stock, guards, liquid providers such as giving milk, transportation, and a select few choice kills for their suburb taste and tenderness. A terrible accident in the distant past caused a tragedy in the "Black Forest" dimension. The area where the earths' ocean waters flows into the dimension had become a touch bigger. This small increase occurred over a large amount of time. The ocean waters constant rubbing against the dimension cloak removed enough of the rubber material to cause this problem. Prior to this incident, the only deadly danger was the acid rain but now they had two enemies.

The fabric tear allows the earth's environment to pass over into the "Black Forest" dimension and cause negative conditions on the "Black Forest" existence. The worse condition causes long periods of drought in the "Black Forest". This period of dryness greatly reduces the safe food supply of vegetation. The drought also reduces the good water in the dimension or dries up many of the good water holes. The drought also causes deadly diseases. The inhabitants get very sick and some even perish from the disease infestation. The drought normally lasts 2 months but has lasted longer many times. This problem is very alarming to the inhabitants as they fear the tear will continue to only get worse.

A couple of the senior superior beings finally agreed that another dimension outside of theirs was causing these destructive conditions in their dimension. They named the intruder "Dearth" which to us is known as "Earth". The permanent fabric tear has remained in its tiny size for centuries but what if it should ever get bigger and cause even more turmoil and destruction. They are convinced that "Dearth" is more than a mere threat and cannot continue to tolerate its interference. The leader remarks to the others that "if there is no "Dearth" then there is no interference."

From this day forward, they would never rest until they could somehow rid themselves of the "Dearth's" co-existence.

CHAPTER 6

Black Forest Habitat"

The incoming earth ocean waters contained grains of land and other particles such as tiny wood fragments. These objects fell to the black forest baron floor before the water froze on the black forest ceiling. The grains of seated land and particles created a fertile ground over the centuries. The fertile ground allowed the development of the black forest habitat.

The canopy trees were the first to appear. They grew extremely fast and tall. The wood filaments attached to the earth ocean land grains absorbed the mineral substance it traveled through and became a very unusual tree type. There were two different canopy trees. One grew fruits and one grew vegetables from the huge canopy top. Each tree top was fourteen feet round.

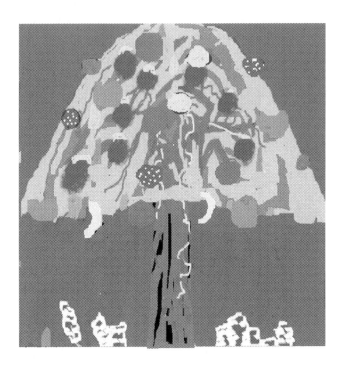

The vegetable tree had strong vines circling the tree all the way to the bottom. The vines grew various vegetables on them. A very big value of the canopy trees was there protection to the "Black Forest" from the "Acid Rain". The canopy make-up was fire resistant and strong enough to resist any penetration from falling liquids or objects. The falling black acid rain that landed on the canopy top would change to pure and clear water and then roll off the canopy. These trees would live and flourish for many, many, years before any life forms would use them. The same holds true for the light tree.

The big and long leafs are sponge like. They would slowly absorb the falling rain drops. The leaf composition mixes with the incoming rain drops and glow for several hours. As the captured rain drops dry so goes the light glow. The glow provides illumination and light. It fades out the same as earth daylight. Six to eight hours of light can be expected from each rainfall. This daylight only covers a mile radius of each light tree. They are very rare and distant from other. Population is popular in these areas because of the daylight time.

Then there were the protruding blades of grass, bushes, flowers, and other growth. This habitat grew and grew and finally became a black forest with partial wonder and filtered air. part of the black forest would always be black from the scaring and burning of the falling black rain.

The damaged habitat would die very slowly because it was very strong. The strength came from the earth land grains. The solid earth grains couldn't absorb the mineral substance as well as the ocean water but the minerals did give extended life to the grains.

The slow dying habitat provided sufficient cover to new growing vegetation in its place. the new vegetation would flourish until the old died out. the new vegetation would then be exposed to the acid rain.

The remaining habitat grew around the large areas of the canopy trees and totally protected from the acid rain.

This habitat received the good rain transformed from acid rain when it landed and rolled off the canopies. The time would come when the canopy trees would provide cover protection to the black forest life forms. Another wonder of the black forest was the air. Air came from the strong and long living unique vegetation.

The pure air would slow the aging process and give extended life to its breathers. The black forest air would give 10 years for every 1 earth year of life. The only drawback was the interference with the earth's negative seeping environment.

"Victor" gathered fallen thread like vines and canopy tree leaves for a very special project. He would use them to make a cover garment to wear for protection against the "black forest rain".

His stay thus far keeps him very close to his canopy tree home as he doesn't want to risk injury or mutation from the "Black Forest Rain" showers. They came quickly without warning and anything exposed was subject to burns from the black rain acidity. Once "Victor" completed his cover garment he would be able to venture anywhere in the dimension and explore its contents. He had already made an umbrella from a "canopy tree" that was sufficient to provide enough cover escape from the black rain until he found suitable cover. He sharpened and shaped the other end of the wooden umbrella into a spear weapon. He still was cautious and did not stray to far from his dimensional "canopy tree" home.

CHAPTER 7

Keeping Track of Time"

Time passes and victor finally stirs and wakes himself. He looked at his watch to see how long he had slept. Noticing the date and year, they set off an alarm in victor's head. How long would the battery last before his watch stopped. His watch was the only way to keep track of time. He immediately made note of how long he had been in this dimension. He was 21 years of age and on his third day in his new world.

"Victor" looked around to find anything he could use to fabricate a way to keep track of time. He found several short logs that were practically hollow from the black rain burn. There were different size vines hanging from some of the canopy trees and also some growing from the ground. He collected a few pieces of charred wood for marking and writing with. He returned to his tree dwelling to work on his project. "Victor" thought of using one of the big canopy tree leaves to hold water. Working with his hands, victor constructed a method which allowed water to drip at a constant setting into a holler log container. He secured the container with vines and placed it under the canopy leaf. He guessed the leaf was strong enough to hold ten gallons of water. He would then have to watch and count the drops for one hour and then mark the log to capture the one hour time. He then made a holler log container to track a 24 hour period (1 day). He made 4 like containers and started each at 6 hour intervals. He would make a permanent mark in a journal he had started previously for each filled container and then reset it. "Victor" wraps his journal in part of a canopy leaf to keep waterproof and weather safe. He then tied a thin strong vine around it and secured the journal around his neck.

Time served no purpose and was simply motionless in the dimension but victor had made a way to keep accurate and precise tracking of time. He felt good about his accomplishment and patted himself on the shoulder as recognition for a job well done.

Time could now be a part of every movement and keep victor aware of his life's position because of his tracking method. The biggest setback was his maintenance connection to his time method. It greatly limited his absence away from his shelter.

Managing this time method was a critical task and one miss of marking time would make his method useless and set time back into its motionless state. "Victor" would remain constantly alert for anything that could improve his time method tracking without requiring his presence. How appropriate he thought that he was named victor. From early childhood he lived up to his name. He never backed down from anything and always welcomed challenge; the more dangerous it was made it more exciting and he would stop at nothing short of being victorious. Fate had changed his path but that was the road he was on anyway. The only difference was that his path was no longer traveled on earth but in another dimension with total unfamiliar makeup. Since someone did have to fall into this dimension, who better than he. He had studied and explored his entire life so that he would evolve into an adventurer equipped with the knowledge and know how to survive any encounter. His big disappointment was the feeling that he would never set foot on earth again or be with any of his family and friends anymore. This is not something he would have bargained for but if it had to happen then he was the best choice. As with the past, he would accept his new challenge and be victorious with his adventures and explorations in this passing of dimension time.

CHAPTER 8

"Victor Finds His First Land Animal"

"Victor" wakes to another day in the "Black Forest". He had conformed to a routine morning ritual of personal hygiene and feeding. He knew how long he slept by the amount of water in the marked water container.

He would venture out a little farther each day until he became fully familiar with the "Black Forest" size, makeup, and contents. Thus far he had only viewed land and water vegetation. he would soon find out that today would be different. There was more than land and water in the "Black Forest".

It wasn't long that he ventured out and found himself vulnerable to sudden downpour of black forest rain. "Victor" quickly evaded the black rain danger by seeking shelter in the holler of a canopy tree. Other unexpected activity from last evening had kept victor from updating his daily journal. This was a good time to do that. He was putting his updated journal away when he detected a light source against the tree wall. Being puzzled and curious he started walking toward the light to satisfy his curiosity. A flash went off and blinded victor for a few seconds. When he recovered his sight he moved slowly and carefully toward the light source. As he proceeded forward he noticed the light was moving. He didn't know he had the light cornered until he came face to face with it. "Victor" was gazing upon a live animal figure shaped like a flashlight and glowing.

It had big eyes that rested on top of the flashlight. "Victor" would find out later that the little creature had hidden legs that it could bring out when it wanted to walk. Its eyes could also close into the head. He could easily keep anything from touching him or causing harm by applying his electric current as an electric fence. He was electrifying. The little fellow was totally mystified at the sight of "Victor". He kept his electric current in a safe mode to allow "Victor" to hopefully touch him. That is exactly what happened.

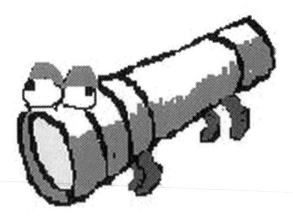

Reaching down, he picked the animal figure up and found it to be extremely nervous but gentle. "Victor" found that when he tightened his grip to hold the little creature its light got brighter. The outer skin was smooth, soft, and without hair. The animal expelled a light ball from itself which fell to the soft ground fungus floor. "Victor" picks up the glowing ball and throws it out of the holler. The glowing ball lands on a hard rock and explodes. The explosion was as powerful or more than an earth grenade was. Talking out loud about how cute and unusual this animal was, victor noticed that the animal understood what he was saying. The electrical makeup of this little fellow converts any language sounds to electrical sounds that he can understand and also talk that language. The animal was very accepting of victor's touch and company. "Victor had found his first pet. He named him "Glow Blow". The black rain had stopped and victor could continue his daily venture but he would now be accompanied by his new pet and friend.

CHAPTER 9

"Saving a Land Animal"

"Victor" was in his fourth year of the dimension. He had saved the life of a black forest bird who naturally became his pet and pal. The birdlike creature was entangled in unbreakable vines and near death from several weeks without food or water. "Victor" found the birdlike creature after he heard a very weak and weird animal call. He was on one of his research hikes and came within a few feet of the tied and hidden creature. He slowly opened the vines from where he heard the sound and revealed the captured creature.

"Victor" was looking at a creature with wings, heavy body fur, round web feet, and a thick round pointed plate on top of its head.

"Victor" slowly and carefully removed the choking vines and set the animal free. "Victor spotted several large egg shaped items on the ground. His inspection revealed an edible egg. Unfortunately, none of the eggs were close enough for the bird to reach and consume. "Victor" finds a heavy object and cracks upon one of the eggs. The egg contained eating substance and fluid. He gave the bird food and water first and then he nourished himself. Both of them now had full appetites.

They both rested for a long time and then awoke fully refreshed and strengthened. The bird reached over and licked "Victor" on the face. The bird then placed his wings around "Victor" and hugged him lovingly. "Victor" knew he now had two pets. He named his new friend, "Roca". This was a Viking word meaning, "one who awoke from the dead". It was applied to those warriors who were badly wounded in battle and not expected to live but they recovered.

"Victor now decided to learn how to ride the huge and very fury "Foca" big birdlike creature. He had the creature to squat down so he could mount it. "Victor" felt extremely comfortable and warm as he settled into the thick fur. He thought how wonderful it would be to make fur clothing. He would later find that the fur replaces itself as it is cut off the creature. He would also find the fur makings being warm in darkness and cool in light. "Victor" rises several feet off the floor and has the bird fly very slowly for a few seconds.

His comfort zone is not yet there so he has "Roca" returned to the ground floor. They both walk back to "Victor's" dwelling. "Victor" will have many flying practices and finally become an expert flyer.

CHAPTER 10

"Discovery of the Black Forest Ceiling Secret"

The black forest ceiling hangs at one mile above the ground floor. Ice prisms are formed from the incoming earth water bleeding through the veins in core deposits leading down and into the black forest region only. Each vein makes its own water color from the minerals in the core deposits they travel through. Each color has its own special power. The power is made from the absorption of dimension core mineral properties mixing with the incoming earth water. The uniting of the earth water and dimension minerals stir a magical formula. The formula produces a powerful potion. The potion becomes effective in liquid form. It is activated by applying a drop to the user left forehead temple. It is deactivated by applying a drop to the users right forehead temple. This occurrence is possible because the beating human pulse from each temple has the right beat to activate and deactivate the applied potion power. (Note: this is the primary reason that prevents the land creatures from effective use of any found color power.) No one is aware of the prisms color power even though they can be captured and used.

Weather patterns sometimes breach the impossible. Violent storms stir the earth water that has occasionally flowed into the dimension with terrific force. The hammering earth water tears tiny fragments from the core. These fragments slowly move downward. They end up on the dimensional ceiling. Only once did a fragment break off and contained all of the color powers. This fragment will change "Victor" forever.

Its magical secret was hidden until the entry of an earth intruder (victor) accidentally found the secret power in one of the ceiling ice prism veins. This accident occurred when victor was learning how to fly on one of the black forest birdlike creatures.

"Victor" and the creature left the ground floor to take their first flight in the "Black Forest" dimension. The ride was so thrilling that they both got reckless and accidentally hit the dimension ice ceiling. the hard pointed head plate of the flying creature broke off a piece of the ceiling. It was the only pebble fragment containing all the water colors and full powers.

There was one other pebble left in the canal that had a few power colors but all the other fragments are of one power color. The fragment was the size of a green pea and shaped like a spear head. The fragment picked up speed as it fell and entered "Victor's" skull from the sharp pointed end. "Victor" became dizzy from the hit and fell off his pet. He plummets to the ground floor and was able to get up. He stands up and finds no bodily injuries. At this time, he doesn't know that the fragment triggered the power of protect-ability. This is why he did not receive any injuries from the fall. In time he would discover his hidden super abilities.

The pet creature quickly landed beside his pal victor. The birdlike creature was very happy that victor was not harmed. He would do everything in its power to see that victor was never harmed. He had accepted victor as his master and now lives only to be with and serve "Victor". They return to victor's home in the black forest where victor prepares a resting area for his pet. "Victor" then lies down to rest and review his recent activities, especially the uninjured fall he had. Aafter several hours of mental review, he finds the answer. He realizes that the ice particle started the entire fall event.

He also remembers something hitting him on top of the head. He places his hand on the top of his head. He can feel a small bump that was not there before. He now knew that the falling pebble was imbedded in his head. Could the pebble be connected to the reason he fell without getting any injuries.

This had to be the answer. The makeup of the pebble had to be the source that protected him. He concluded that somehow the pea size pebble gave and took the protect-ability power. But why did he have and then lose the protect-ability he asked himself? He reviews his fall and remembers thinking, "How can I protect myself from getting serious injuries" while falling.

After landing he no longer had that thought. He concluded that the pebble had the power of protect-ability and he could turn it on and off simply by thinking that. "Victor" then wondered if any of the other ceiling ice prism colors contained a power source. There was only one way to find out. He would have to revisit the dimension ceiling and so he would.

CHAPTER 11

"Black Forest Inhabitants"

The "Black Forest" was unoccupied by inhabitant beings for many ages. The closest organism to an inhabitant was the creature known as "Water Head". "Water Head" started out as a water organism and developed into a round Water Head Pole. There were many other living micro water organisms but only one "Water Head Pole". A rock shifted during one of the high tide ocean water entries into the dimension. The unusual and one time rock shift created a brief small vein. The small vein quickly closed as the ocean current returned the rock to its previous position. The "Earth" ocean water that did enter was trapped in the small closed vein. The small vein was the only one crossing other veins as it descended to the "Black Forest" ceiling.

The trapped water mixed with various mineral deposits which created a much different power effect. It finally settled on the ceiling like the other veins do. Unlike the other vein paths, one of the minerals in this vein kept it warm enough that when the water entered the ceiling a little kept going as falling rain into one of the "Black Forest" pond waters. One of the pond living organisms "Water Head Pole" received a direct hit and swallowed a large amount of the special tonic water before the rest dispersed, diluted, and lost most of its power in the pond waters. Over time, this pond living organism would evolve into the first and only water creature called, "Water Head". It would have a big round head and fish like body shape without scales and feed on the pond water banks.

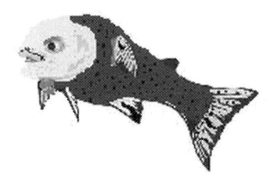

There was a time when a devastating rain poured down on the "Black Forest" and flooded everything. This rare occurrence was caused by the warming of the ocean waters entering the dimension on the high tide. a lot of the volcanoes on earth had erupted and spewed their boiling lava over the earth and the oceans. This catastrophe may well have been the reason for the extension of the dinosaur age.

The volcanic lava and ash poisoned the air and either burned or choked the life out of the greater part of all the earth and the dinosaur". Some of the earth plants were immune to destruction and broke away from their burned ground cords. These were extremely rare plants that produced a fluid that enhances living organisms. They floated and passed from earth waters into the dimension. They found their way down and through the dimension ceiling where they settled on the edge of the water where "Water Head" lived and ate. The "Earth" lava kept the plants hot enough that they melted the ceiling ice and passed through. The torrents of rain finally stopped and the "Black Forest" gradually returned to its normal existence in its twilight dimension.

"Water Head" soon found the plants which had all broken up and rotted except one. These rare plants had somehow lost their immunity in the dimension. "Water Head" entered the cracked plant and drank the remaining fluid. This was the last plant of its kind.

The rare fluid had mixed with human sweat, dropped by those passing by the plant and created a special portion. Unlike any other plant in the dimension, this earth plant formed a humanistic structure on its receiver. As with any of the unusual dimension occurrences, it took a very long time for this change to happen. Nature had decided to remove this plant species from existence. The power of this plant was twofold and permanent. It changes the internal and external organism makeup giving its receiver the capability of gaining intelligence equal to that of an average earthling. It would have limbs that grow and produces a figure in the form of a human; thus, emerges our intelligent water head creature into the first and only land being. His name would be "Blender".

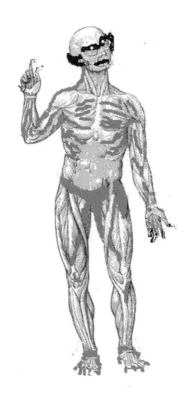

The power change also requires the receiver to breathe like a human and the land being starts to gasp for clean, open air.

It didn't take newly gained intelligence to realize the new land being had to get out of the water and up on the land; like real fast.

"Water Head" retained hidden gills that would allow him to breathe and live in the water for months at a time before emerging from the water to breathe needed air. He obtained this breathing condition when he was changed but being the first time he had to breathe air from the newly developed openings made it hard to breathe in and out.

This new experience frightened "Water Head" who felt like he was dying and forced him to resist which made the change more difficult.

There were two genetics that remained with "Water Head" when converted to the new figure. One was its ability to reproduce itself.

The land creature had the ability to start this process at will. It takes some time to reproduce and the land being can also stop the process at will. This land being was a makeup of both male and female properties. The other genetic that remained with the converted "Water Head" was its overall gel look. This gel made up the outer shell of the land being. The gel shell was thicker than our human skin. It gave the impression that the land creature was transparent. This transparency is simply camouflage which creates an illusion of seeing through the land being. The body shell gel allows the land being to blend in with any feature and look invisible.

Much like the earth's caveman, the "Black Forest" land human would slowly evolve over time. Its mind was only 2% of a human baby's mind. It would wander alone for a very long time before it gained enough intelligence to realize its reproduction and camouflage capability.

The land being would always remember how it came about and in time start thinking and craving answers to unlimited questions.

Would the future ever come when the land being would realize what the plant fluid had done, and if so, what effect would it have on this new arrival? Once a "Water Head" and now transformed into a human shape figure called, "Blender".

"Blender" wandered alone for a long period. During his mental and physical development, he became stronger and stronger. He had traveled the "Black Forest" all the way to the end which then exposed a baron dimension.

"Blender" also ventured into the baron dimension. He found the baron dimension was much bigger than appeared from the outside.

As he rested for his return trip home, his thoughts wandered and he dreamed of the baron dimension being the covered homeland that gave protection from the awful black acid rain. His faculties had become highly developed, as humans were, and he was ready to start populating his selected home site. He chose the furthest point of the black forest because of the abundance of water to use. New inhabitants could live in the water and also on the land when necessary. This site would be the new world for "Blender's" land creatures as it comprised the "Black Forest", abundant water, and protective cover.

The appearance of a baron dimension went deep and far enough to make any onlooker believe that's all it was. Blender knew differently. there were changes in scenery and other interesting sights if someone did enter far enough.

There was a time when the long loneliness of being the only inhabitant took the desire for living out of "Blender".

"Blender" hadn't developed very much at that time and had no real sense of right reasoning or desire of belonging. He saw the baron dimension as completely desolate and dead. He would end his frustrating existence by going as far as his energy would carry him and allow the baron dimension's mouth to swallow him whole. Even if he did change his mind and want to live his weakness would not allow him to travel back far enough to survive.

He moved deeper and deeper into the baron dimension.

Suddenly he started to notice changes in his surrounding that appeared to his liking. What he saw renewed his belief in life.

His curiosity became more focused than ever. There was a narrow opening to his left. He went through the opening and immediately found himself almost floating off the floor.

The wall within this baron section had wart like protrusions. This part of the baron dimension had very little gravitational pull. He found that any pressure upward would take him off the floor a few inches. The harder he jumped made him go higher and further. He threw a small stone and watched it go a distance that took it out of sight. This was a great and unusual find.

He explored the area and found it to be rather small (about the size of five earth football fields). "Blender" felt that this area had great potential but he couldn't quite say what it was at this time. (He will later decide to make this the entertainment arena. Those who earned rewards would receive free tickets to the games and rides later to be created.) He would keep this find a secret until he had reason to do otherwise. He now wanted to return to the "Black Forest" and start his family. "Blender" immediately turned on his pregnancy genes to begin the birth of living and breathing inhabitants. "Blender" knew it would take some time (later he would learn about time and that the time for a birth is one month) to give birth so time was extremely precious. Since the dimension had no rotation and set in a fixed and still position, time worked differently than that on earth. Five years was the equivalent to one earth year. "Blender" returned from the baron dimension with five newborn inhabitants. (Newborn inhabitants are five years old at birth; as such, they can take care of themselves. This releases "blender" from the baby care time period.) Since "Blender" initially wanted to perish in the barren dimension, he did not bring a lot of food and water.

His weakness and thirst had exceeded its limit when the first born occurred. He had no choice but to sacrifice his first born. With great sadness he turns the first born into needed food and liquid.

This not only saved "Blender" but also the other four newborns. Each newborn inhabitant is born with the ability to immediately understand speech and carryout "Blender's" wishes. They are born with only two percent intelligence but quickly gain more in short time spurts. These conditions make it much easier for blender to care for them. He works to keep all alive as they depart the baron dimension.

The remaining living organisms except one absorbed the lesser power of the remaining plant fluid from the pond. Each of these organisms would evolve into other "Black Forest" land creatures. There were also fish from earth in the "Black Forest" ponds. These fish came from incoming fish eggs in the earth waters that breached the dimension. Those fish in the pond with "Water Head" would change their shape and makeup to become the "Black Forest" water creatures. A few would also have the ability to live in and out of the water. A couple would have the ability of flight. A smaller water organism was transformed into a figure shaped flashlight. This new creature was transformed differently from "Water Head" and able to breathe and live in and out of the water.

This new creature preferred the land to water mainly because of its abilities. This creature appeared very impressive to "Water Head."

The unusual creature had swallowed some of the more potent plant fluid before it withered and faded away. This occurrence gave the organism the ability to think and talk in addition to the other altering changes it received.

The creature's head was shaped like earth's flashlight. It had the power of light. It could turn on and off at will. It could increase its light as needed. The remaining body was round and very warm.

The internal bone system had been mutated into a living generator source. The brain was the switch that fed continuous electrical waves to the bones. The bone system was connected to the head and fueled the light source. The creature would release small balls containing excess energy to prevent an overload that could harm if not kill it. The balls would lose their energy like our earth batteries do. While energized, the balls could be exploded by hard impact. The explosion was equivalent to earth grenade or dynamite depending on how hard they were hit. The creature gave off a dim glow in the dark and was called, "Glowblow". "Glowblow" was the first water creature found by "Victor".

Even in the dimension, nature takes care of its own. All of the water creatures would retain enough of their gills to allow them to stay under water for several months before needing air. The creature's instinct automatically took them to living under the water. When they came up for air they used the time to visit the "black forest" and collect essentials to take on their return to the water. Their water home also gave protection from the unknown destructive "Black Forest Rain" showers. Some of the creatures will be found to be scared, maimed, and disfigured from exposure to the black acid rain. Their low intelligence prevents them from sensing danger, reasoning, etc. Their only thought is to return to their water home to escape the danger. In doing so, they don't think about using cover and stay exposed while in pursuit to return home. While on land, the water creature's instinct has them avoiding all other living things. They stay hidden and unknown until victor makes contact on his first outing in his protective leaf garment.

The land being's found many plants and foliage. They discovered that the living ground leaves were green and gave healthy nourishment and good feeling.

This green leaf was able to grow and flourish under the protection of the large and wide "Canopy Trees". The dead foliage was black from exposure to the "Black Forest Rain". They found other foliage outside the canopy trees to be of different colors and having unusual effects on the receiver. These plants were extremely rare and very well hidden. They were very tiny and concealed by the larger charred and/or dead foliage. This concealment also protected the plant from the black rain. The new plant appearance took a very long period of time for the occurrence to finalize itself from receiving one water drop of their color from the "Black Forest" ceiling ice color prisms. The power in each color was changed on its fall through the black acid rain floating filaments. The drops absorbed the black rain acidity which altered the power within. Although the ceiling is frozen ice, a drop will slowly occur and fall to the ground floor.

It takes a very, very, long time for each drop to form, slide, drip, and drop to the "Black Forest" ground floor. Being of special makeup, the drops immediately give undetected plant growth that cannot be harmed from exposure to the black acid rain. The below list identifies the altered power in each color:

1. **Telepathy**: (light blue) ability to communicate with each other silently.
2. **Healing**: (light gold) ability to radiate the power color into its own minor wound or infection and cure the condition.

(Note: the healing properties could not work on severe injuries or diseases such as the scaring received from the acid rain.)

3. **Protect ability**: (light gray line around the entire body): the gray line contained a property that would repel solid items that touched it.

4. **Levitation**: (light yellow): ability to lighten the body weight and float several feet above the ground. One can move twice as fast in this mode.

5. **Speed**: (light red): ability to speed up body metabolism to allow movement at twice the normal walk or run speed.

6. **Duplication**: (light orange): ability to grow a lost limb.

7. **Camouflage**: (light brown): the receiver could take on the appearance of its surroundings at will and blend in to look invisible.

8. **Light green**: causes color blindness until the dark gray power is consumed.

9. **Vision**: (dark orange): power to see double the normal distance.

10. **Strength**: (dark yellow): power to apply twice the normal strength.

11. **Breath**: (dark gold): ability to release air four times the amount of normal air.

12. **Imprisonment**: (dark brown): those charged with crimes not punishable by death were placed into a motionless state by injection of this color. (Note: the motionless state was the equivalent of death). Only a select few were given this authority by the leader, "Blender". Anyone else found using this color would be put to death by injection of the dark red color which only blender had control of.

13. **Shape**: (dark blue): gives the ability to alter oneself into large and aggressive known animals in the dimension.

    The body would return to its normal self in several hours or earlier if the inhabitant desired to. Some evolved fish turned into such animals that looked like our earth wolves, cats, bears and dogs.

14. **Color vision**: (dark gray): Consumption of this color would return the color eye sight to one that was made color blind by the light green color.

15. **Food**: (dark green): The receiver of this color will not desire food for two weeks as the dark green color generates body substance as replacement for food intake.

16. **Death**: (dark red): The lead inhabitant "Blender" declared this power control to himself only. He would use it as the penalty for those who committed labeled crimes. The intake of this color was painless and caused immediate death. One such crime was the possession and concealment of this color. The guilty party would receive no mercy for this crime as the injection was immediate. Note: there was a three day period after death that the victim could be returned to life and only blender knew how to do this.

There were two other colors mixed with the dark red and then injected into the skull to regenerate brain and organ activities that restored the dead to life.

The land creatures were very disturbed to find that the plant powers were severely weak and short lived due to the twilight (permanent darkness in the black forest). Usage would turn the internal body fluid plant power(s) to poison and cause sickness and sudden death; as such, the plants were

totally useless without sufficient light. Light was the source needed to have full plant power and life without damaging or killing the land being's. The entire land population was informed of this danger and forbid to ever be seen even touching it.

The penalty was death to show all how important it was to adhere to this law. The offender would be made motionless in a cage below the water and perish from drowning once it needed to rise to the surface for fresh air. (Note: The land beings would stop breathing and perish if they stayed motionless for more than a day while under the water. Putting the offender on exhibition for all the others to observe would show the severe and horrible death mode for tampering with the color plants. The action is rarely needed but when used it reminds the entire population to comply or die. (Anyone possessing a power will turn to that color and be easily noticed.

Some with little intelligence will try a power on believing they will keep it and survive. Others try and find ways to remedy the sickness and death but none have ever been successful.)

CHAPTER 12

"Victor Revisits the Black Forest Ceiling"

"Victor" is awakened by his bird creature licking him in the face. "Back off" he replies in a loud voice. The bird creature "Roca" moves away in confusion. It was only reaching for attention from its friend and master. "Victor" pats "Roca" on his head to show his affection. He then looks at his water watch to see how long he had slept which showed 10 hours. "Victor" was more tired than he had realized. He tended to his personal hygiene followed by his fruit breakfast and then feeding "Roca".

"Victor" thinks of the earth sun with its warmth and light and solely misses it. This black forest with its black forest rain makes for a dark and dismal climate and surroundings. He makes himself content but will never get use to living in this environment. He waits patiently for the time when he can somehow return to earth.

Until that time comes, and he was positive it would, he would continue to search, learn, and find out as much as possible about this hidden dimension he had fell into.

Today was going to be a good day he thought to himself. "Roca, "Glowblow", and myself, would embark on another venture to the black forest ceiling. This time would be different. He was prepared to gather a piece of each ceiling color ice and place in its own container. "Victor" had collected numerous round tree branches that he hollowed out for containers. He made stoppers from the same branches to fit each container. The container would preserve each ice color as it melted. Later, he could take his time to examine each and hopefully expose its secret.

"Victor" puts "Glowblow" on his side. He then mounts "Roca" and sets off to the ceiling above.

Being a mile high and shadowed by the "Black Forest" darkness conceals the beautiful color prisms of ceiling ice. As victor approaches the ceiling he is even more amazed than his first visit at the beauty he sees. His ordeal on his first visit took his attention from the ceiling and was ended quickly. He grabs "Glowblow" and squeezes to intensify its light. He flies "Roca" very slowly and close and takes his time to view the various colors of prism ice. He then has "Roca" to carefully hit precise spots to break the different colors of ceiling ice. As each color falls, he catches it and immediately places it in its own container.

Having captured one of each color ice piece, victor returns to his "Black Forest" domicile. Previously, "Victor" had dug into one of the higher tree crevices and made a safe and secure storage place to protect his wooden containers. No sooner than he had finished securing the containers did a downpour of "Black Forest Rain" start. He was always amazed at the instant scaring and destruction the acidity of the "Black Forest Rain" made on everything it touched except the canopy tree and its leaves. "Victor" had collected pieces of the "Canopy Tree" leaves and thin vines that occasionally fell off and onto the ground. He had been working on a cover garment to fit each of them. This last collection would be enough material to complete the cover garments. They would then be protected when exposed to the black rain. They would be able to move freely in the "Black Forest" while anything else would have to stay fixed in place until the "Black Forest Rain" stopped. "Victor" realizes that the garments will only be effective until the leaves dry up and die. He would make other garments to be ready for use when needed.

This would give victor temporary chances to find other hidden inhabitants if such did exist. They would not be able to evade his presence during these periods of "Black Forest Rain". It wouldn't be long before he completed these covers.

Everything was done except sewing a few more patterns together. For now he was going to relax with his friends, and listen to the "Black Forest Rain" as it puts him to sleep.

CHAPTER 13

"Secret Powers Uncovered and Unleashed"

According to his structured water time device, victor spends the next six months experimenting with his water colors. He performs test after test on each to uncover the secret power ability. Victor had toiled for months and months with some success. His diligent research and experiments resulted in the find of nine different water color powers. The remaining seven water color powers could not be found. It might take years before he uncovers the power secrets but he would never stop trying until he totally succeeded. He continued his work on his nine power color discoveries. He applies each on himself to unveil the affect. He found it almost unbelievable but true about the powerful abilities in the water colors. The excitement kept him so nervous that he found it very difficult to make the copious notes he had to capture and preserve.

His next step was to label the containers to identify each of his new found powers. ("Victor" doesn't realize that he already possesses all the powers even though each did reveal itself when he applied it.) He was finally looking at his documented "Black Forest" ceiling ice color prisms finds. **These were the incredible mystical powers he had captured.**

1. **Telepathy**: (light blue) ability to communicate with all living things. Language would adjust to the language of the receiver for easy understanding.
2. **Healing**: (light gold) ability to radiate the power color into the wound, draw, then absorb the infection and mend the condition to its previous healthy state.
3. **Protect ability**: (light gray line around the entire body): the gray line contained a property that was invincible to anything that touched it.
4. **Invisibility**: (light yellow): allows invisibility if the body cells are vibrated and intensified to that point of acceleration.
5. **Speed**: (light green): ability to speed up body metabolism to allow movement at desired speeds.
6. **Duplication**: (light orange): ability to clone one image of himself.
7. (light brown): the super ability to pass through objects.
8. (light red): not discovered yet
9. **Vision**: (dark orange): power to see endless miles and through all objects of solid wood, metal, rock, and liquid.
10. **Strength**: (dark yellow): power to apply any degree of strength at will.

11. **Breath**: (dark gray): ability to release unlimited amounts of powerful air.

12. **Flight**: (dark green): the power color changes the inner body to an unnoticeable and harmless composition which allows immunity to gravity. the composition generates electrical energy through all the body veins which gives flying skills. a side effect also allows the release of controlled electrical discharges through the finger tips.

13. (dark blue): not discovered yet

14. (dark gold): not discovered yet

15. (dark brown): not discovered yet

16. (dark red): not discovered yet

He surmised that the water color ingredients mixed with body ingredients made a chemical that became the color power ability.

The main drawback was that the water colors could only be applied and used one at a time. Whenever he tried to apply two or more they would create conflict and make all ineffective.

His persistence in continuous multiple applications finally prevailed. He had tried almost all combinations before finding one that worked. He mixed the four light water colors together and applied a drop to his left forehead temple but nothing happened. He pondered briefly and decided to take a sip.

Feeling faint made him scared but it quickly subsided and victor felt super incredible. He jumps for joy and finds himself way up in the top of his home "Canopy Tree". He hadn't realized that his excitement vibrated his body cells and gave flight to him when he jumped with enthusiasm. He picks some of the fruit and returns to the ground floor with ease and without injury. He yells, "success!" How sweet it is". He repeats the test and mixes the five dark water colors together and had the same success but with different powers this time. Thinking how any two or three combinations didn't work but four and five did convinced victor that four or more of the light or dark colors would work. He smiles and thinks to himself how fortunate he was to have had the lifestyle and education that fit perfectly into his current circumstances.

His survival and many accomplishments thus far would not have been possible had he been raised as the average earth person or without the extensive education and exploration he had harnessed before falling into the dimension.

Minutes, hours, and days pass. "Victor" still has all of his known and unknown new powers. He was convinced that they were permanent until he deemed otherwise. He soon found out differently. He wakes one morning in pain and very weak.

He can hardly move. He immediately realizes the powers had become poison overtime. (He does not know the real reason.

All of the previous excitement disturbed his metabolism and upset his inner body balance; thus, causing a temporary pain and weakness which would have passed on its own.) He touched his right forehead temple and removed the powers. This saved his life. He was fully cured in a short period. Not knowing how long he had to wait to be safe before applying the water colors again, he decided to wait several days. His waiting period was over and victor was more than ready to regain his power abilities. He takes a sip of the combined water colors mixture and instantly feels his returned super powers. He didn't know exactly how many days he could keep them before letting them go to prevent another painful ordeal. He set up a separate 24 hour water time device to keep accurate track of his power rotation. Over time, "Victor" finds that using one water color at a time can last months without any danger to him. He is very pleased because victor feels very comfortable when he has the power of protect-ability.

This was great news to victor as he no longer had to wear the protective leaf suit in the "Black Forest Rain". It was very restrictive and bothersome.

The time had come and victor would be in control of this dimension. His goal was now to prepare for his return to earth but not as victor. He had to return as a totally different person because he actually was different. He was now a super person and ready to dawn his new mission in life.

He would live for the preservation of earth. he would take the name of "Rainbow".

"Victor" chose this name because of the many power colors and his encounter with the "Black Forest Rain". Only he would know the meaning of his alias "Rainbow" and how the "Black Forest Rain" dimension changed his life.

CHAPTER 14

"Victor Rescues a Land Creature

The day had come for "Victor" to test his new powers. The "Black Forest Rain" was falling and he wanted to take advantage of this occasion. He places "Glowblow" on his side and leaves his "Canopy Tree" cover for the first time without his cover garment. The "Black Forest Rain" was coming down but rolling off "Victor" without any harmful effects. He was equipped with the light color water powers of telepathy, healing, protect ability, levitation, speed, and invisibility. (He still doesn't realize his possession of all powers yet.) Being invisible was going to allow him to see without being seen should he encounter any living dangers. As "Victor" moved forward he could smell the black ash taking the place of beautiful foliage, vegetation, wood, and anything else touched by the "Black Forest Rain" except himself and "Glowblow". This was a fantastic outing. "Victor was very familiar with the area he had thus far traveled many times before in his cover garment. The cover garment gave him protection but prevented him from seeing except straight ahead.

Anything could have easily avoided his sight. He guessed that if there were any living things they were fearful of him and kept their distance.

"Victor" decides to make haste with his speed power and move to the end of the "Black Forest" wherever that may be.

He arrives at the end of the "Black Forest" and sees that it stops where the dimension caves start. He darts in the caves for a few seconds but sees that there is nothing but baron dark space so he quickly returns to the "Black Forest". He would have found "Blenders" cave but it was well hidden with camouflage by the land creatures.

The remaining caves were small and desolate and nothing as unique as the one "Blender" found. The "Black Forest Rain" is still falling as "Victor" moves through new territory. He detects the noise of many voices. He wondered if he was imagining sounds or were they really real. He heads toward the sound and gazes on his first sight of ten living beings residing under a "Canopy Tree". They all had the shape of humans. How could this be possible! He ventures into their camp undetected by his invisibility and listens to their chatter. His telepathy lets him understand what they are saying. One talks of the leader "Blender" setting an example of another who had made contact with forbidden color plants. He had been found lying in the forbidden color plants and assumed by the others to want consumption. The captive being tried in vain to convince them that he had accidentally tripped and fell into the color plants.

He was actually trying to free himself from the color plants entanglement when the others found him. The mere fact that he was mixing with the color plants was enough for the leader "Blender" to take immediate action. He could not show the slightest sign of forgiveness for this act.

He had to show them all that there was no mercy for anyone when it came to the color plants.

The human shaped being was being held at the other end of the camp. "Victor" moves to that location and finds the poor being hanging upside down from a "Canopy Tree" vine and dripping body fluids from punctured wounds. The wounds came from objects being thrown and some poked at him from the others.

All at once the air is filled with silence and the human shaped beings are standing still looking in one direction. "Victor" looks in that direction and sees a being with a much larger shape approaching the others. They all start yelling "Blender". "Victor realizes that it's their leader. "Blender" walks over to the wounded being, grabs his top hair, and abruptly raises his head. He tells the others to look upon the being and remember the example he would be for making contact with the forbidden plant colors.

"Blender" explains to them that the being would die in the under water cage.

This would show the entire population the consequences of disobedience to this strict law. He then told them to prepare their collections for return to their underwater home after the "Black Forest Rain" stopped.

There was a lot that "Victor" couldn't understand but he couldn't let this poor being continue to be constantly tortured much less killed. He slowly moved closer and closer to the captive being. He did not want to make any noises that would alarm the others. He reached the captured being that could hardly move. "Victor" uses his telepathy to convey his actions to escape with the captor. He quickly unties and releases the captor who drops to the ground almost lifeless. Even though the captive being is very slim and tall, he is still quite heavy. "Victor" wishes he had his power of strength. The next best power was "levitation".

Strapping the arms of the captor around his neck, "Victor" slowly rises off the ground floor. His rise is very, very slow because of the added weight but he manages to rise above the reach of the others. Suddenly he hears a loud response from the leader "Blender", "the captive being must have consumed some of the color plants because he has the power to escape our grasp". "Victor" doesn't understand how the leader could detect the escape so quickly.

He would find out later from the captive being that their population has telepathic ability and picks up on his communication with the captive being. "Victor" struggles to levitate outside of the "Canopy Tree" and into the "Black Forest Rain".

The strain was so intense that "Victor's" vibration slowed down and made him visible. This revelation showed the inhabitants leader what bad really occurred.

Somehow the stranger had recently discovered the powers within the "Black Forest" color plants. Only "victor" knows the real truth; his powers come from elsewhere. This new awareness of the stranger changes everything thought the leader. They had been patient about capturing the stranger because they wanted to observe his movements and actions to better know him. They could have easily captured him but not now. The "Black Forest Rain" was slowing down which was an indication that it wouldn't be long before it stopped. "Victor lowers them to the ground and keeps the escaped being close to him for protection from the black acid rain. He also regains his invisibility as the weight strain is much, much, less. He needed every remaining second to distance them from the others whose vengeance was at its peak. "Victor's" luck had run out. The added weight of the inhabitant he was carrying greatly weakened his speed power.

The "Black Forest Rain" also stopped. The enemy could now easily plunge upon them. There is nothing else "Victor" is able to do. The enemy is aware of "Victor's" presence even though he is now invisible and aims to capture both. A shadow appears overhead as the enemy approaches "Victor". In a flash, "Victor" finds himself and his luggage removed from capture.

"Roca", his birdlike friend had become impatient. He was worried about his master being out in the "Black Forest Rain" for so long. "Victor" had made a cover garment for "Roca" who had worn it previous times with "Victor". (His body was resistant to the black acid rain but he wore the garment because it pleased his master). "Roca" guessed that his master would be searching much farther and so he flight was to unknown areas of the "Black Forest".

He spotted his master and other being near capture and scooped them out of harms way. "Roca" then returns all of them to his master's home.

After arriving unharmed, "Victor" makes the inhabitant comfortable and rewards "Roca" with lots of hugs. "Roca" is very pleased with his reward from his loving master who he loves and worships. He accepts each hug with total delight.

Before the wounded inhabitant wakes up in awful pain, "Victor" decides to try his power of healing. Placing his hand on each wound, "Victor" watched as they healed themselves.

All the wounds turned out to be minor enough to allow the healing process to take place. When the inhabitant woke up, he had dreamed of being cured by "Victor". "Victor" told him it was real and not a dream. He explained his powers to the inhabitant. The inhabitant tells "Victor" that he is forever in his debt for all that he has done. The inhabitant knows he can never nearly repay for what "Victor" has done but he would compensate by being his permanent servant if he would so allow.

"Victor" knows the inhabitant can never return to its own kind and is now an orphan. "Victor" says he would be honored to have the inhabitant as a companion.

The creature made a gesture as if to say he would serve "Victor" untill death. He was very tall. He was born with only one ear. "Victor" names the inhabitant "Slim".

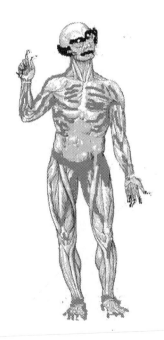

CHAPTER 15

"The Earth Threat to the Black Forest"

The primary protection to the "Black Forest" was its dimensional secret. The dimension was its own paradise. The uncanny connection to the earth breathed life into this lifeless dimension but also presented a possible threat to its stable existence. Preservation of its secret was finally compromised with the accidental entry of an earth being. The life cycle of the "Black Forest" within the hidden dimension was now threatened by an outside source from the "Earth".

The earthling was totally unaware of his negative impact on the "Black Forest" until long after his stay in the hidden dimension. He had disturbed the natural order of the inhabitant's life cycle. His prowling and probing explorations stirred up the relaxed and comfortable living mode they had enjoyed for centuries.

Now they were having feelings they never had before. They felt fear and danger from the earth intruder. The awareness of the stranger's powers only heightened their discomfort and threat. Their leader, "Blender" decided they had to rid themselves of this invasive enemy before the normal order of life as they knew it and enjoyed was disturbed even more. As such, they found themselves making protective weapons and devices conceived from the higher intelligent elders. They also started using camouflage techniques to evade the earthling. The leader, "Blender" had the ability of camouflage built into his gene structure which gave the idea to the others. It wasn't long before the wild animal destructive desire arose in many of the scared and disfigured inhabitants. These beings were already mad and ill-natured because of the "Black Forest Rain" damage and ugliness they had to bear. The acidity in the black rain drops had taken its toil on many of the land creatures and habitation.

The black acid rain was one enemy they could not fight but rather retreat from and hope for the best. By the time some of the inhabitants gained the courage to make contact with the earthling, "Victor" had acquired the powers of new and would be impossible to capture, much less get rid of. Following the earthling back to his dimensional home and keeping constant observation on his movements did uncover a weakness. The leader, "Blender" noticed the super side of the earthling only lasted a short time before he returned to a normal earthling. This weakness would give the inhabitants the means to rid themselves of this strange and unwanted invasion. (What the land creatures didn't know was that "Victor" always has his powers but puts them in remission when not needed.)

The inhabitants could never understand and stayed confused and puzzled by the destructive actions of the invader. They witnessed the invader cutting and burning their habitat many times. The invader was always digging holes and tearing up vegetation to expose the bare ground.

These and other mysterious actions of the invader convinced the inhabitants that this was a serious and severe threat to their "Black Forest" and had to be removed permanently.

CHAPTER 16

"Escape From
the Hidden Dimension"

While the inhabitants were preparing their capture, the earthling was preparing his escape from the dimension. The inhabitants would fail in their capture because the earthling would escape first. "Victor" approaches his big birdlike creature "Roca" and pets him affectionately. He tells "Roca" he will have to remain in the dimension because he would be too conspicuous on earth and never accepted by the humans. He explained to "Roca" that he would be better off here with his other birdlike creatures. "Roca" moans with grief but understands and accepts his fate. Unlike "Roca", "Glowblow" was one of a kind and looked like an earth flashlight. He could easily blend in on earth. "Glowblow" would never forget "Roca" and was extremely thankful that he was going with "Victor". The earthling, "Victor", had completed his packing and started moving toward the place where he had fallen into the dimension. It was time for the rare dimension to open the portal to earth.

"Victor" remembered that it would only stay open for a brief time so he had to move fast.

The leader of the inhabitants, Blender" had formed a small number of talented inhabitants and was in pursuit of capturing the earthling when they witnessed the escape. They watched in transfixed amazement as the earthling made his escape. Using his powers of strength and flight, the earthling secured his friend "Glowblow" and with his possessions rose upward until they disappeared out of sight from the inhabitants below. "Blender" notices the bright light above where "Victor" is heading too. He makes a mental image of this location and occurrence as the light disappears and the portal closes. "Blender" realizes he has found the light needed to work with the forbidden plant colors. He didn't know if the portal would open again but he wasn't going to take any chances. He would keep a guard posted here at all times and immediately report to him when any change occurred. "Blender" was going to stay as close as he could too this location to prevent missing the next portal opening. In the meantime he would prepare as the earthling had done. One thing still puzzled "Blender" about the earthling; how could he have the powers without getting sick and dying. This was a question that "Blender" would keep very close to himself to search for until answered.

"Victor" continued to rise until the portal finally came to the point of exit where he had entered from. "Victor" couldn't believe his eyes but knew it was real. The portal opening to earth was very narrow. "Victor" had to push his packs through first and then he and "Glowblow" could go through and return. He then took a "Canopy Tree" leaf from his bag and held it in the portal entrance as it closed and again disappeared. The "Canopy Tree" leaf however didn't disappear; the part unstuck was still visible and would remain a permanent marker should victor ever return. He used the "Canopy Tree" leaf because it couldn't be destroyed by wind, rain, fire, or other impact.

Looking around, "Victor" could see very little change from when he left this place in the "Grand Canyon". He could still detect the remains from the fire and smoke he was part of. He imagined that in the years gone by this area would be covered in new grown brush, trees, etc. with no signs of ever being disturbed. He would find out later that he was only gone for one year.

"Victor" departs the "Grand Canyon" undetected and returns to his island home. He is greeted by his parents "executor". The island had been abandoned.

"Victor" was told by the "executor" that his parents were killed in a plane flight headed towards the "Grand Crayon" in search of "Victor". They knew he had gone on an expedition in a particular area of the "Grand Canyon" but he was long overdue for his return. Thinking the worst, his parents decided to fly out and find him. This ordeal would brand guilt in "Victor's" mind forever because if he had never left his beloved parents they would be alive today. The "executor" explained to "Victor" that he had been on many other expeditions and apart from his parents and island home for long periods of time. His parents were always patient and respectively waited for his return. Why they reacted like they did was going to remain a mystery and "Victor" was sure not the fault for their death.

The "executor" then gives "Victor" the keys to the island and bank accounts. "Victor" finds he has inherited enormous wealth in the billions and billions of dollars and his island paradise. The "executor" was the closest uncle to "Victor" and his parents. He was also a loyal friend and lawyer for his parents for over 40 years. He never had children and lost his wife several years before. "Victor" asked the "executor" for his continued loyalty, friendship, and companionship. "Victor" also asked the "executor" to administer the financial affairs and island care and maintenance. "Victor" would give him total decision making authority. There was good reason for all of this and "Victor" took the "executor" into his confidence to keep his secrets. The "executor" had always looked upon "Victor" as a son anyway and told him it would be his honor and privilege to act in the place of his departed parents. "Victor" was and still very fond of his last living relative and would call him "Uncle".

As expected, "Uncle" was intrigued by the dimension stories and pet "Victor" had brought back. "Uncle" was in his late seventies and not nearly healthy enough for "Victor" to ever consider applying any of the water color powers to him for surely they would be instant poison and death. The same would have happened to "Victor" back in the dimension when the water colors changed to poison. The water colors immediately start to turn poison on entry into the body system. Being young gave "Victor" the time he had to use the powers in a safe mode before the poison started taking affect on the body. "Victor" also had a very large body frame and extremely muscular even before falling in the hidden dimension. Exercise was a normal living condition on his island home and his life style of adventure and exploration was a contribution to his bulk. The poison would immediately permeate the body and cause death to an already weakened elderly person that "Victor" surmised older than sixty. (What "Victor" doesn't know at this time is that the magic water colors have lost their power. The different environment on earth and lack of the continuous nutrients from the dimension ceiling causes evaporation of the main ingredients that keep the power effective. "Victor's belief in the process he uses to apply the powers is worthless because he possesses all the powers and can use at will).

"Victor" told his "uncle" that his new place in life was to be a "caretaker of earth". He wanted to do this without being noticed, thereby preventing suspicion in his direction. Intrusion into his island and life would only make for a bad situation and danger to his "Uncle". One of his water color powers was the ability to create intense vibration to his body cells which would alter to body invisibility. "Victor's" training so far allowed him to easily apply and control three water colors at one time.

Two would normally be "Invisibility" and "Protect-ability". The third would be the power needed to remedy the opposing obstacle. "Victor also needed a costume that would identify with his new image. He would be called "Rainbow". He chose this name because of all the many power colors. The letter "r" would show on his chest suit to signify his other self. No one would understand the significance of this "R" or the name "Rainbow" except himself and his "Uncle". He would wear a belt that had color containers around it to hold the different water color powers. During times when he shouldn't apply the combination colors, he could freely select an individual water color from his belt. He would simply push the container underside button to get a drop of water and apply to his left forehead temple. He would diffuse by touching his right forehead temple. None of this would be needed if "Victor" knew he possessed all the color powers and they are

Printed in the United States
By Bookmasters